COPY 26

J
Fiction   Shreve, Susan Richards.
              The flunking of Joshua T, Bates / by
          Susan Shreve ; illustrated by Diane de
          Groat. -- New York : A. Knopf, 1984.
              82 p. : ill.   3-5

              SUMMARY: Driving home from the beach
          on Labor Day, Joshua receives some
          shocking news from his mother: he must
          repeat third grade.

              ISBN 0-394-96380-6 (lib. bdg.) : 9.95

          1. School stories.

This is the story of Joshua T. Bates,
who was held back in the third grade
even though he was a lot smarter
than Billy Nickel or Tommy Aiken.

It is also about a teacher
who knew that was unfair,
and did something about it.

The Flunking of
JOSHUA T. BATES

Susan Shreve

Illustrated by Diane de Groat

Alfred A. Knopf
NEW YORK

For Caleb

This is a Borzoi Book
Published by Alfred A. Knopf, Inc.
Text Copyright © 1984 by Susan Shreve
Illustrations Copyright © 1984 by Diane de Groat
All rights reserved under International and Pan-American Copyright Conventions.
Published in the United States by Alfred A. Knopf, Inc.,
New York, and simultaneously in Canada by
Random House of Canada Limited, Toronto.
Distributed by Random House, Inc., New York.
Book design by Mimi Harrison
Manufactured in the United States of America
1   3   5   7   9   0   8   6   4   2

Library of Congress Cataloging in Publication Data
Shreve, Susan Richards.   *The flunking of Joshua T. Bates.*
Summary: Driving home from the beach
on Labor Day, Joshua receives some shocking news
from his mother: he must repeat third grade.
[1. Schools—Fiction]   I. De Groat, Diane, ill.   II. Title.
PZ7.S55915Fl 1984   [Fic]   83-19636
ISBN 0-394-86380-1   ISBN 0-394-96380-6 (lib. bdg.)

The Flunking of
JOSHUA T. BATES

One

On Labor Day, driving home from the beach, Joshua's mother told him that he was going to have to repeat third grade.

"Nope, I'm not," Joshua said when his mother told him quietly so his miserable older sister, in the back seat of the bright blue van, wouldn't overhear, although of course she did.

"I've already been in third grade once," Joshua said very reasonably.

"Of course you have, darling, but the teachers feel that you're too young for your class. You need another year to mature."

"I am very mature," Joshua said crossly. "What do

they expect at nine years old. A beard?"

"They expect you to be able to read, Josh," Amanda said helpfully from her perch in the back seat. She was reading a fat book with small print just so Joshua's father would say to his mother, "Isn't Amanda a fine student." And his mother would sing back, "Just wonderful, wonderful, wonderful."

"You're a jerk, Amanda," Joshua said to her. "I hope you grow up to be a third-grade teacher and that your hair falls out."

"I'm going to be a surgeon with long hair, which I'll wear in a French twist when I'm operating on people." Amanda crossed her legs like a woman, so she looked to Joshua very much like a forty-year-old reading teacher with buck teeth and sunglasses. He wanted to bop her but resisted.

"I want to be a crook," Joshua said fiercely.

"That's quite enough," his father said crossly, settling into his customary bad humor for long car trips with children. "Get in the back seat, Josh."

Joshua did. He lay in the far back of the van and played with toy soldiers on his stomach. Geor-

gianna, in her baby carseat, took a soldier and put it in her mouth. Then she took her wet pacifier with traces of applesauce from lunch and stuck it in Joshua's mouth.

"Josh baby," she said happily.

"You bet," Amanda said.

"Please," their mother said.

"Will Joshua have to repeat third grade all year?" Amanda, with her usual bad judgment, asked pleasantly.

"Not any of the year," Joshua said, taking matters into his own hands. He leaped on his sister's back and tore one of the pages of her thick book. He was crayoning her face with purple Magic Marker when his mother scrambled between them in the back seat.

"This is an awful time for Josh," she said to Amanda. "Leave him alone."

"He doesn't need to kill me; it's not my fault he can't read."

"He didn't kill you," their mother said.

Very sweetly, she took Joshua in the front seat with her.

"Sometimes I think about Amanda falling by accident into a sewer and floating to Delaware," Joshua said to his mother as he leaned sadly against her and watched the trees whip by his window. Already the leaves were tipped with red, promising the beginning of school.

"Why didn't you tell me about third grade in June?" Joshua asked. "Didn't you know then?"

"I knew, but I didn't want you to have all summer to be upset about it."

"If I'd known, I would have left home in June. Now I have only one night to pack up, and all my clothes are dirty."

"I'm sure that after the first week, you'll find it's not so bad to be in third grade again."

"It won't be bad at all because I'm not going to be in third grade again. By Halloween I'll probably be in East Africa."

Joshua climbed over the front seat, stepped on Amanda's bare foot as hard as he could, and lay down on the back seat with his soldiers.

The Bateses were on their way back home from the beach after two nearly perfect weeks at the ocean. Joshua had fished and swam and crabbed and sailed with his father. At night they had sat up late, eating dinner by candlelight, listening to the ocean pound like thunder on the dark shore. His father told stories. His mother read to them. Even Georgianna, chomping on her pacifier, listened. Some nights Amanda, sweeter than he'd ever seen her, played Chinese checkers or Monopoly or gin rummy until Joshua's eyes, heavy with sleep, closed and his father carried him off to bed.

Mornings at the beach, he'd occasionally wake up with a terrible dread like a black hole dug suddenly in his stomach while he was sleeping and remember school. And how he hated it. And how he'd have to go back and back and back year after year until he had feet the size of his father's.

Especially he had hated third grade.

Mrs. ▓▓▓ was the third-grade teacher. According to stories Joshua had heard from past third graders, she had been hired to teach at Mirch Elementary after she won first prize for Child Hating, Especially Boys, in a contest sponsored by Peanut Crunch Natural Cereals.

"Josh-u-a," Mrs. Nice had said to him every morning right after recess. "Did you happen to memorize your spelling words?"

"Yes," Joshua would begin. "I memorized my spelling."

"Next time you had better memorize all of the words and not just half of them," she would say, smiling her grape jelly smile, flapping his spelling paper in her hand so no one in the class could possibly miss the big red 50 at the top. "Now, Joshua," could you read the paragraph you practiced for me?"

And Joshua would read, blushing the color of apples, halting at every word. The terrible class would giggle and whisper and give one another knowing looks. Even Billy Nickel, who couldn't read either.

"And what about your composition on a favorite holiday?"

"I don't have a favorite holiday. I love every single day I'm not in school and I hate every day that I am. *I quit third grade.*"

And he had picked up his book, his spelling, his composition with "My Favorite Holiday" written on blue-lined paper, and dropped them in the teacher's wastebasket at the front of the room.

Of course, he was back in Mrs. Nice's classroom the following day. His mother didn't believe his stomachache or his flu symptoms or the tumor he was certain had developed in the back of his knee during the night. What his mother did believe, quite rightly, was that Mrs. Nice was not fond of children, especially boys, particularly Joshua T. Bates. And she told Mrs. Nice exactly that.

In return, Joshua promised that he would stick it out in third grade and not quit again.

He had meant he'd stick it out for one year. That was that. A deal's a deal.

"You lied to me about third grade," he called to his mother from the back seat of the blue van. He was lying on his back with ten dead Confederate soldiers and two living ones on the battlefield of his stomach. "You promised."

That night his mother tucked him in bed, where he settled with his Matchbox cars, forty-six metal soldiers in different positions for shooting, and twelve stuffed animals.

"Did you lay out your clothes for tomorrow morning?" his mother asked.

"I won't need clothes in East Africa. They wear bones in their heads and go naked."

His mother took pants and a polo shirt and socks from his top drawer and put them on the table next to his bed.

"I'll try to get you a chicken bone in the morning." She kissed him good night. "I'm very sorry about third grade, Josh."

"Me too." He turned on his side so the metal cars wouldn't stick in his back. "Please don't tell me life is full of these kinds of disappointments like you usually do."

His mother laughed and ruffled his hair. "At least you won't have Mrs. Nice for third grade again. You'll be in the other class with Mrs. Goodwin. Do you remember her?"

"Oh, great," Joshua moaned. "You'd have to be blind not to remember Mrs. Goodwin. She looks exactly like a military tank."

"I understand that for a military tank, she is a very good teacher," his mother said. And then she explained to Joshua the reasons for his flunking the third grade. Some children, boys especially, she said, grow up more slowly than others. Which doesn't mean they aren't just as smart; in fact, one day they will catch up, maybe even sail ahead of their friends. But for right now, she told Joshua, he was one of those slow-developing children who hadn't learned to read well enough to keep up with his classmates.

"It's a question of eye-hand coordination, Josh," she said.

"I was the best baseball player in third grade. My eyes and hands coordinate fine."

"For baseball but not for reading yet. Soon, I promise, you will be reading as well as you play baseball."

"Not with Mrs. Goodwin," Joshua said crossly.

"I think you'll learn to like Mrs. Goodwin, Josh," his mother said as she kissed him good night.

"Not a chance," Josh said.

Joshua tried to put himself to sleep with wandering dreams of Mrs. Goodwin. In one dream she had arms like an octopus, only thousands of them, full of spelling books and remedial books and reading books, S.R.A. material. He couldn't even see her face. In another dream she carried a pitchfork everywhere, even to the ladies' room, with Joshua seated on the top of the spears. When she gave directions for tests, her voice had the low rattle of a city squirrel and he couldn't understand a word she said, even if she repeated the directions.

In the morning he didn't eat breakfast or kiss his mother good-bye. When he saw Amanda examining her dimples in the hall mirror, he called her by a name he wasn't allowed to use.

His father, trying hard to be pleasant, said he would walk Joshua to school.

"I think I'll walk alone," Joshua said, needing some time to plan his trip to East Africa.

"We'll both go with you," his mother said brightly, guessing, as she always did, that he was not going to school at all but planning to leave the country.

"Do you think I'll stop by People's Drugs and play Pac Man instead of going to school?" he asked as they walked down Rodman Street with his mother on one side and his father on the other so he felt like an escaped juvenile delinquent who couldn't read.

"It crossed my mind," his mother said, taking his hand. "And in a way, Josh, I wouldn't blame you."

Just to confirm his worst fears, there was Tommy Wilhelm walking into the fourth-grade classroom as Joshua walked into Mrs. Goodwin's class with his parents.

"Joshua T. Bates!" Tommy Wilhelm called at the top of his lungs. "You're going into the wrong room."

Joshua didn't answer.

"What's the matter, Josh? Did you flunk third grade?" Tommy Wilhelm shouted again.

For one moment before he entered the third-grade classroom and saw Mrs. Priscilla Goodwin sitting behind her desk, Joshua had a terrible thought about what he would do to Tommy Wilhelm on the playground. And then Mrs. Goodwin got out of her chair and, without even a trace of laughter on her lips, walked toward Joshua and his parents.

She looked, with her broad, compact body, exactly like a military tank, as he had remembered.

"Brother," Joshua said and before he knew it, his

parents had slipped like ghosts out of the room and he was left there to face Mrs. Priscilla Goodwin advancing on him all by himself.

Two

Mrs. Goodwin was a small, square woman with curly gray hair, thick, wire-rimmed glasses, and a serious face which at that moment seemed to Joshua fierce enough to wipe out a battalion of metal soldiers with a single glance.

"I'm Joshua Bates," he said.

"I know," she replied, shaking his hand.

On the bulletin board behind Mrs. Goodwin's desk, there was a sign painted in bright colors: WEL-COME TO THIRD GRADE.

"I suppose you know that I've been in third grade once already," Joshua said as he sat on the edge of one of the desks.

"Today is the worst day in my life," he added com-
batively, hoping she would consider herself at fault.

"Mine too," Mrs. Goodwin said matter-of-factly
as she wrote the date on the blackboard. Joshua
wanted immediately to ask her why, thinking perhaps it was his arrival in the third grade that had
ruined her life as well as his, but the other children
were beginning to arrive so he said nothing. He
slid into one of the desks in the front of the room,
took a pencil and paper out of his bookbag, and ap-
peared to be hard at work on cartoon drawings of
Star Wars figures. He hoped no one would recog-
nize him.

"That's a good place for you to sit so I can keep an
eye on you," Mrs. Goodwin said as she placed a red
reading book titled *The Joy of Reading: 3* on his
desk.

Joshua didn't bother to tell Mrs. Goodwin that he
wasn't going to be around to keep an eye on. She'd
find out soon enough.

Instead he looked at *The Joy of Reading,* which
was the same book Mrs. Nice had made him read
one terrible day after the next.

"I've had this book already," he said. "I know these stories by heart."

Mrs. Goodwin looked at him crossly over her wire-rimmed glasses.

"Recite them," she said.

"Not by heart exactly. You know what I mean." He leaned back in his chair and with his eyes closed, he imagined the pleasure of throwing the warm, soft tomatoes rotting in his mother's garden at Mrs. Goodwin's gray print dress.

The classroom began to fill with children whose faces were familiar to Joshua from the playground but whose names he did not know, of course, since it was a matter of principle at Mirch Elementary to know only the names of the older children, never the younger ones. These children were smaller than Joshua had imagined possible. He felt like a huge, dumb grizzly bear, he told Amanda later. Not one of these third graders came to his shoulder.

At the desk next to him was the smallest girl Joshua had ever seen in grade school, or so she seemed. She had pale pink cheeks, tight yellow curls, and a foolish-looking dress with aqua hippopotamuses all over it.

"Are you actually in third grade?" he asked her. Certainly he wasn't going to spend the year with a girl so young that she still wore zoo animals on her dresses.

"Of course, dummy," she said quite pleasantly. "I remember you from last year. You've been in third grade once already."

"No kidding," the boy in back of her said. "Did you flunk or something? I have a cousin who flunked third grade twice."

"I didn't flunk," Joshua said, glaring at the tiny boy. "I'm just visiting. Tomorrow my family is moving to East Africa."

By the time the final bell for school had rung and Mrs. Goodwin's class was full of the smallest people he had ever seen gathered together in the same room with him, Joshua had developed a serious stomachache and asked to be sent to the school nurse immediately.

"After the spelling test," Mrs. Goodwin said as she passed out paper for the first spelling test of the year.

"I may be dead after the spelling test," Joshua

said, but he took the test anyway, scored a 50 as usual, and asked to be excused to go to the boys' room.

The hallway of Mirch Elementary was empty. He walked diagonally across to the fourth-grade class-room and looked through the window of the door. There, right in front of him looking like the enemy on TV, was Tommy Wilhelm, and behind Tommy was Andrew Porter, Joshua's best friend from Mrs. Nice's class, the only person in the whole world that at this moment in his life he liked a bit. Including his parents.

Bravely, he opened the fourth-grade classroom door, walked up to the desk of a new teacher hired that year to teach fourth grade, and said that he had to see Andrew Porter immediately. It was an emer-gency.

"How come you're not in this class, Josh?" some-one called from the back of the room.

"He flunked," Billy Nickel, the only seriously stu-pid boy from Mrs. Nice's third grade, said thought-fully. "My mother told me last night."

"That's a lie," Andrew said.

"I saw him go into Mrs. Goodwin's class with his

parents this morning," Tommy Wilhelm said. "I don't think he was going to a birthday party."

"Please," the new teacher said, rising from her desk. "It's time for social studies."

"I'm actually moving away," Joshua said as loud as he could, which wasn't very loud because his voice was filling with tears.

Andrew agreed that Joshua Bates was telling the absolute truth. He knew, he said, because they were best friends. "His father told me they were moving last night on the telephone."

"Liars," Tommy Wilhelm sang out as Joshua left the classroom with Andrew Porter.

In the empty boys' room Joshua started to cry in spite of himself.

"I mean, Billy Nickel was ten times worse at reading than me," Joshua said.

"I know," Andrew agreed sympathetically. "And so were Tommy Aiken and John Starer."

"And Dickie Fluger."

"It's unfair," Andrew said sadly.

"So I'm running away. Blowing town. Beating it.

Mrs. Goodwin is a tank," Joshua said, feeling his strength return.

They leaned against the windowsill. The window was half open, over the playground full of kindergarten children swinging and playing in the sandbox.

"Where'll you go?" Andrew asked.

"East Africa."

"Alone?"

"Do you want to come?" Joshua asked brightly. "We could have a really good time."

"Well," Andrew said. "Probably I can't. My parents wouldn't let me."

There was a knock on the bathroom door and Mrs. Goodwin called in her low, gravelly voice.

"Joshua? Are you all right?"

Joshua didn't answer.

"Joshua?"

"I'm not dead if that's what you mean," he replied.

"We better go," Andrew whispered. "I don't want to spend the day with the principal." He reached into his pocket and took out two plastic standing

Union soldiers with rifles pointing. "You can have them," he said. "They're extras. I'll see you on the playground in an hour."

Back in the classroom Joshua told Mrs. Goodwin that he had the flu and needed to go home pronto or everybody else in the third grade would catch it.

Mrs. Goodwin put her hand on his forehead. "You're not hot," she said. "You'll last until three o'clock."

"You'll be sorry," Joshua said darkly.

"We'll see how you feel after reading," Mrs. Goodwin said. "I need you to help me in reading class."

So Joshua stayed through reading class, moving his chair next to the child in the hippopotamus dress, who needed special help with phonics.

"I won't read aloud, you know," he said to Mrs. Goodwin as she passed his desk.

"I wouldn't dream of asking you," she said.

During social studies Mrs. Goodwin asked Joshua to explain about the lives of Indians on reservations, which he did. She didn't mention the fact that Joshua knew about Indians because he had already studied them in third grade once. She simply acted as if Joshua T. Bates, formerly retarded, was the smartest boy she had met in several months.

By recess Joshua had almost forgotten his stomachache and was helping a new boy from Peru add three digits.

As he left the classroom to go to the playground, Mrs. Goodwin called to him.

"I'm sorry to hear you have to leave town tomorrow," she said.

He shrugged. "Who knows? Maybe my plans will change."

Amanda was out on the playground hanging by her knees on the junglegym when he came out for recess.

"H'lo, Josh," she called to him upside down. "How's Mrs. Goodwin's class?"

"Not bad," he said. "I'll probably be promoted next week," he lied.

Three

Tommy Wilhelm was already on the playground with Billy Nickel, who should have been the one to flunk third grade, and two other enemies of Josh's from third grade. They were in the corner of the playground, leaning against the cyclone fence with criminal attitudes, and Joshua could tell without a shadow of doubt that they were talking about him. In all probability they were saying how he couldn't read and had an irregular brain, had never learned to spell, and would grow up to be a trash collector in Japan.

Courageously, Joshua sauntered down toward the cyclone fence, looking at the sea of faces on the playground, wishing that Andrew were somewhere in sight to help him out.

"I brought a softball and bat if you want to play baseball," he said to Tommy as he leaned on the fence beside him.

"Big deal," Tommy said.

"Why not? The field's empty," Billy Nickel said. "We could have two teams."

"G'won if you want to play. Myself, I play with fourth graders only."

Joshua could feel his blood shooting like hot darts straight through his arms, but he didn't say a word.

"See you later then," he called, slinging his bat over his shoulder.

"Andrew's looking for you," Amanda, still hanging red-faced by her knees, called to him. She pointed in the direction of the lower field, where Andrew was walking with two friends.

Joshua caught up with them, batting Andrew lightly on the shoulder.

"Want to pitch?" he asked.

"Sure," Andrew said. "You guys against us," he told the two boys he was with. "We're up at bat first."

"Tommy Wilhelm is passing it around school that you flunked, " one of the boys said as he took the softball from Joshua.

"Tommy misunderstood," Joshua said as patiently as he could. "There was a mix-up. The fact is if I stay in town, I'm being promoted very soon."

They played all during recess until the bell, and Joshua felt better than he had felt in twenty-four hours, since he had first heard from his mother about third grade. He hit one home run and a double. He caught a fly ball and a grounder and tagged a man out on first base. He was actually beginning to feel normal when Tommy Wilhelm, followed by Billy Nickel and the two enemies, waddling like ducklings behind Tommy, sauntered over to the lower field.

"Third graders aren't allowed to play with softballs. Only rubber balls," he called. "School rules."

Joshua was up at bat with two strikes. He tried not to listen to Tommy Wilhelm. He imagined himself hitting the ball *smack*, sending it out beyond the pitcher, over the heads of the outfielders, a home run. But when the ball came straight as a dime over home plate, he swung hard and missed.

28

Perhaps if Tommy Wilhelm hadn't laughed a loud monkey laugh that went on and on, Joshua wouldn't have dared to hit a boy one head taller than he was, flanked on either side by three allies built in large solid squares like cement blocks.

But Joshua didn't think.

As soon as he heard Tommy Wilhelm laugh, he took off at a sprint, running as fast as he had ever run, charging like a tiger or a bear or an elephant— so Amanda told their parents that night at supper— straight into the center of Tommy Wilhelm, knocking the wind out of him. Tommy toppled over like a sack of flour suddenly emptied.

"I can't breathe," he moaned.

"You killed him!" Billy Nickel shouted, hopping on Joshua's back.

"Not yet," Joshua said.

"You're just a third-grade bully," one of the enemies said, and he pushed Joshua into the cyclone fence.

"I'm not in third grade," Joshua said. He fell to the asphalt, with both arms pinned behind him. "I just got promoted."

One enemy hit him in the nose. Another kicked

him hard on the side. He might have been brain-damaged, as he told his parents later, if Andrew had not flown out of nowhere, sailing bravely into the center of the fight.

"I'm telling," Andrew said.

"Josh hit Tommy first," Billy Nickel said.

"Tommy was teasing, and look what you've done," Andrew said, pointing to a wave of blood pouring from Joshua's nose down his face. "Murderers."

A teacher came rushing over and then another. The principal, called from his desk by one of the enemies, took Joshua by the arm.

"I'm going to have to call your mother," the principal said as he led Josh back to his office. "Violence on the playground is not permitted."

His mother wasn't home when the principal called. By a stroke of good fortune his father, who was not inclined to be good-tempered on these occasions, was out of the office.

"Go back to Mrs. Goodwin's class and write, 'I will not fight on the playground' one hundred times," the principal said.

Mrs. Goodwin was sitting at her desk, looking less like a military tank at that particular moment than a soft-fleshed grandmother with a kindly face.

"H'lo," Josh said. He sat down at his desk.

"Trouble?" she asked.

"I started a fight on the playground and the principal is trying to reach my parents to send me home. For violence."

Mrs. Goodwin raised her eyebrows.

"Who won?"

Joshua shrugged. "There were four boys against me," he said. "I'm glad I'm leaving the country."

Mrs. Goodwin got up from her chair with *The Joy of Reading: 4*, pulled up another chair next to Josh, and opened the book on his desk to the first story.

"I lied," he said to her.

"What was the lie?"

"I said you were promoting me soon to fourth grade."

"Not soon, Josh," she said thoughtfully, "but maybe before the end of the year if you work hard and don't leave the country."

Four

Joshua stopped at People's Drugs to play Pac Man on the way home from the first day at school. Billy Nickel was already there with Tommy Wilhelm, standing in line for their turn. Joshua stood behind them.

"So?" Billy Nickel asked. "Did you get suspended or not?"

Joshua didn't answer.

"At this rate, you'll be twenty-one and driving before you get out of third grade," Tommy Wilhelm offered pleasantly.

Joshua picked up a *Dr. Strange* comic from the newsstand and pretended not to hear.

"What's the matter? Scared to talk?" Billy asked after he finished his turn.

Joshua dropped his fifty cents into the Pac Man machine and concentrated on the blue and yellow figures on the screen. He played on and on, winning and winning.

"You know your friend Andrew?" Tommy Wilhelm asked. "He's not long for fourth grade. Right, Billy?"

"Right," Billy said.

Joshua bought a double-dip chocolate ice cream cone at the counter, and the copy of *Dr. Strange,* and walked home along Wisconsin Avenue.

"I spoke with the principal," his mother said when Joshua got home. "He is very cross."

"I hope he drowns in the Potomac River," Joshua said, giving first Georgianna in her playpen and then the cat, Plutarch, a lick of his ice cream.

"He said you initiated a fight and beat up Tommy Wilhelm."

"I didn't beat him up enough," Joshua said.

"He's suspending you for tomorrow."

"Good," Josh said. He sat on the living room couch and put his feet up on the coffee table. "Either I will play Pac Man all day or else go to East Africa tomorrow. I haven't decided which."

His mother picked up Georgianna and bounced her absently on her lap.

"Please, darling, don't call attention to yourself by getting into trouble."

"I would have been very glad not to have any attention at all today. Tommy Wilhelm called attention to me and I wish I could turn him into vanilla pudding."

"If you have that kind of attitude, Josh, repeating is going to be much harder."

"Well, that's the attitude I've got."

The front door slammed open and Amanda rushed in.

"Josh got in a terrible fight," she called from the hall. "He attacked four boys and almost beat them single-handed."

"So I've heard," Mrs. Bates said.

"News gets around fast," Josh said.

"Are you suspended or not?" Amanda asked. She

sat down on the couch next to Joshua, who had set up an army of metal soldiers, plus Andrew's plastic ones, on each extended leg.

"Suspended."

"Too bad."

"It's not too bad at all. It's going to be wonderful. I'll have all day to do nothing at all like it's a vacation. Perhaps I won't even have to leave town if I can get suspended often."

"What about your reading if you're not in school, Josh," Mrs. Bates asked impatiently.

"I'll teach Josh to read," Amanda said.

"I already know how to read, you dolt," Josh said, leveling a whole army of soldiers by brushing them off his leg.

"What I mean is we can read together," Amanda said with surprising good sense.

And then she boxed him gently on the arm and said, "You were amazing today."

When the telephone rang, Mrs. Bates thought it was Mr. Bates calling from the office to say what time he'd be home for dinner. Amanda thought it was her friend Luli calling for the homework assignment in language arts. And Joshua was sure it was Tommy Wilhelm's mother calling to whine about injustices.

Instead, to everyone's surprise, it was Mrs. Priscilla Goodwin, calling to invite Joshua over.

"For tea," Mrs. Bates said.

"She didn't mention tutoring?" Joshua asked.

"She simply said tea and cookies," Mrs. Bates said.

Joshua shrugged. "Well, I guess I'll have to go see the military tank if she insists," he said.

But in truth, he was very pleased.

Five

Joshua knew absolutely what he was going to do about school as he took his dirt bike out of the shed, rode it up Lowell Street, passed the older boys playing street hockey, and screeched to a halt so the wonderful bike reared in the air like a stallion at the stop sign on Thirty-fifth Street.

He rode down Wisconsin Avenue on the sidewalk, taking the bumps full speed, his wheels spinning on the pebbles. At R Street he turned left to the address Mrs. Goodwin had given, a rectangular house with red geraniums in pots at all the windows, and there she was on the front step waiting.

"Hello," she called.

"H'lo." He locked his bike on a wispy birch tree in front of her house, bounded up the steps, and followed her through the front door.

Certainly he knew that it wasn't going to be possible for a boy of almost ten to leave home and travel alone in East Africa, whatever the emergency. Besides, he would miss his family, even plump Georgianna banging her spoon on the high-chair table and splashing her dinner on the walls. Neither was he going to be able to arrange to be suspended on a regular basis. Besides, what he wanted more than anything except a black ten-speed bike was to be promoted to fourth grade as a perfectly smart boy who could spell and read, not brilliantly, of course, but well enough. And was good at sports. Next he wanted to capture Tommy Wilhelm in a gunnysack, dress him in girls' clothes, perhaps a hippopotamus dress with puffed sleeves, and tie him to the flagpole in front of Mirch Elementary for everyone in the world to see.

Joshua sat down at the table in Mrs. Goodwin's kitchen, took a stack of slender brown-edged sugar cookies, and filled his teacup with milk and sugar and a small amount of tea.

"I want you to make me as smart as anyone in the fourth grade," he said matter-of-factly.

"You are already smart, Joshua. What you need to do is learn to read."

And so together they made a serious plan of action.

Every weekday afternoon Joshua would go first to People's Drugs, play two games of Pac Man to relax, then get his bike and ride to R Street, where he and Mrs. Goodwin would sit at the kitchen table with cookies and tea, chocolate as the weather chilled, and practice reading and spelling until the words fell like magic into stories in his brain.

On that first afternoon Mrs. Goodwin showed him all around her house. She took him to the library stacked with books from floor to ceiling; on the desk was a picture of Mrs. Goodwin looking young and thin, even pretty, with two small smiling boys on her lap. There was a yellow Labrador retriever, who had already lived one hundred and forty people years, lying in front of the fireplace, as still and patched with age as the oriental rug on which he slept. In a cage in the window of the living room, a brown mother finch sat smugly on two tiny eggs. And in an aquarium, visible as day, an unattractive boa constrictor shot his forked tongue at Joshua as he peered through the glass.

"The snake belongs to Mr. Goodwin," Mrs. Goodwin said. "I hope he'll take the awful thing to his new apartment as soon as possible."

"Are you moving?" Joshua asked.

"Mr. Goodwin is moving," Mrs. Goodwin replied, and Joshua could tell she was not anxious to discuss Mr. Goodwin at greater length.

On the way home Joshua decided, however, that Mr. Goodwin was responsible for the first day of school being the worst day in Mrs. Goodwin's life, as she had told him that morning when they met.

Andrew was waiting on the front steps when Joshua got home from Mrs. Goodwin's that first day. He was dressed in the same shorts and T-shirt he had worn to school, only the T-shirt had a stripe of dried blood and the flesh just above his cheekbone was as purple as a ripe plum.

"Are you going to be promoted soon?" Andrew asked.

Joshua shrugged.

"Maybe, and maybe I'll move away. I haven't decided. How come?"

Andrew pulled his baseball cap down over his forehead, wiped at the dried blood on his T-shirt.

"Because there's a new rule at school."

"What's that?" Josh asked.

"No fourth grader is allowed to have friends in the third grade."

Joshua took a piece of Doublemint chewing gum out of his pocket and split it with Andrew.

"Says who?"

"Says Tommy Wilhelm."

"So?"

"So he beat me up for being your friend," Andrew said.

"Brother," Joshua said. "I guess it's a lucky thing I got suspended for tomorrow."

And he sat down on the front steps next to Andrew, wishing he could erase the whole last year and return to the time when he was a regular third-grade boy with a reputation as an athlete and not a problem in the world except cavities.

Six

Andrew agreed to walk to school with Joshua, as they had always done when they were in the same grade.

"As far as Thirty-eighth and Idaho," Andrew said sheepishly. "And then you go down Thirty-eighth and I'll walk across the field to Mirch so no one will see us together."

"I guess that's okay," Joshua said but he didn't really mean it.

"I know I'm chicken but I can't help it," Andrew said. "Tommy Wilhelm could squash me with one hand if he made up his mind to it."

"Not me," Joshua said, and the more he thought

about Tommy, the more determined he was to be promoted to fourth grade as soon as possible.

One afternoon at Mrs. Goodwin's house, waiting for the sweet brownies in the oven to cook through, Joshua told Mrs. Goodwin about Andrew and Tommy Wilhelm.

"I can't even count on my own best friend," Joshua said.

Mrs. Goodwin took the brownies out of the oven and put a hot one on a plate for Joshua. She took two brownies for herself and sat down in a chair next to Joshua with *The Joy of Reading: 4*.

"I know exactly how you feel," she said. "Sometimes the only person you can count on is yourself."

"Have you ever had a best friend let you down?" Joshua asked.

"For a very long time Mr. Goodwin was my best friend," Mrs. Goodwin said softly.

"And now he won't even take his stinking snake away. Right?"

"That's right," Mrs. Goodwin said, and they both laughed.

By late September, Mrs. Goodwin had made Joshua her permanent assistant in the 3X classroom. He read with the bottom reading group, helping the children with phonics. He showed the new boys who had not had multiplication how to multiply and worked on arithmetic facts with flash cards. He helped the girls build a tepee in the classroom, building most of the frame himself. He was the captain of the third-grade softball team, the best player in the class.

"So what?" Tommy Wilhelm said when Paulie Soll, one of the new boys in 3X, told him about Joshua's athletic skills. "Of course he's good. He's a year older than everyone and twice the size of most of you."

"You're probably jealous of Josh," Paulie Soll said to Tommy and then reported the conversation to Joshua.

"You bet," Tommy Wilhelm said. "I always wanted to spend the rest of my life in third grade."

But the fact was that in a matter of weeks, Joshua Bates had become the most respected boy in 3X. Obviously he was smart, they all thought, because Mrs. Goodwin needed his help with the other children. Certainly he was the best athlete. He had taught Paulie Soll multiplication and Janie Sears three-digit addition and Sally Stone to sound out words phonetically. Everybody wanted to sit next to him in music and art class, where there was a choice of seats. He was chosen to play the part of Daniel Boone in the class play, *Mercy, Be Kind to the Indians*, and he was the only third grader to memorize the entire poem "Casey at the Bat" and recite it in assembly.

By October no one in third grade cared a bit that Joshua Bates had flunked.

In early October the fourth-grade softball team challenged the third-grade softball team to a game at recess.

"Tommy Wilhelm wants to cream you," Andrew said. "He has had it in for you ever since your fight on the playground. He's told us to stop at nothing."

The game was a good-spirited one, an even match until just before the recess bell when the score was four to four and Joshua was up at bat with one person out on the third-grade team.

He hit what surely should have been a home run. He ran easily past first, into second, but just as he came to second base, Billy Nickel put his foot out and Joshua sailed over second base stomach down in the dirt and was tagged out.

"He was tripped," Paulie Soll said.

"I saw it," Sammy Laser said, pointing to Billy Nickel. "He did it on purpose."

"I did not," Billy Nickel shouted. "Joshua Bates is a third-grade klutz. He tripped over his own feet."

Joshua picked himself up off the ground, wiped the dirt off his bloody knees, and walked to homeplate.

Sammy Laser, the smallest boy in 3X, was up at bat.

"I'm batting for Sammy," Josh said.

This time he hit a groundball that slid right through Tommy Wilhelm's hands at shortstop, right past Billy Nickel at second base, and surely would have been caught easily by Andrew if he had not at that very moment screeched at the top of his lungs

that a bee had stung him on the elbow and started dancing wildly around the outfield.

So, just as the final bell for the end of recess rang, Joshua ran around the bases, sliding into home plate, and the third grade won five to four.

"Did you get stung badly?" Joshua asked Andrew on the way home from school that day.

"There aren't any bees in Washington in October, you dolt," Andrew said happily.

Seven

On October 11, Joshua was ten years old. He woke up on the morning of his birthday feeling perfectly terrible, wanting, as he told his mother later, to sleep all day.

Birthdays in the Bates family were occasions for great celebration, and for days before the actual date Joshua had been having mixed feelings about being ten.

"Happy birthday," Amanda sang as she rushed into his bedroom while he was still under the covers. "Turn over for ten spanks."

But Joshua pulled the covers over his head.

"Beat it," he said in a voice Amanda recognized immediately as serious.

"Brother," Amanda said, going into her parents' room. "Don't go out of your way to say happy birthday to Josh."

When Mrs. Bates knocked on Joshua's closed bedroom door, he said, "Don't come in. I'm dressing."

"Since when has Joshua worried about dressing?" Mr. Bates asked on his way downstairs.

Mrs. Bates shrugged.

"Happy birthday, darling," she called through the door, but Joshua didn't respond.

"Josh?" she called again.

"I'm still dressing," he said.

In the mirror over his dresser, he looked at his face to check for significant changes since yesterday when he was nine. He had to bend down to see himself in the mirror, which his mother had hung when she redecorated his room for his seventh birthday. He looked, he decided, very much the same as the day before except bad-tempered which he certainly was.

Everybody was at the kitchen table for breakfast when Josh came downstairs. His mother was making scrambled eggs in the electric frying pan with her back to him and didn't bother to turn around. His father was reading the sports page as usual and Amanda was counting the friendship pins she had gotten that week.

"One hundred sixty-eight in all," she said happily.

"One hundred sixty-eight friends?" Mrs. Bates asked.

"One hundred sixty-eight close friends," Amanda said absolutely.

"Brother," Josh said. "I only have one close friend." But no one seemed to have noticed when he slipped onto the bench next to his father except Georgianna, who bopped him pleasantly on the head with the salt shaker.

"Some of the children in Mrs. Goodwin's class are still eight," Joshua said crossly.

"Not very many," Mrs. Bates said. She served a plate of eggs to everyone including Georgianna, who dumped hers carefully upside down on the high-chair tray.

"Enough," Joshua said. "Nobody is ten. Nobody in the entire third grade including Molly Beaker, who is mentally retarded."

"Pretend you're nine today," Amanda said as she fastened the rest of the friendship pins to the tie of her left tennis shoe.

"What a terrific idea." Josh said crossly.

"We don't need to celebrate your birthday, Josh," Mrs. Bates said.

"What about presents?" Amanda asked. "I bought a present for four ninety-five, not including the tax, at Snyder's on Saturday."

"Well?" Mrs. Bates asked. "What do you think, Josh? You could spend this year without a birthday."

"I like that idea very much," Joshua said. He cleared his plate and put it in the dishwasher.

"No party tonight?" Mr. Bates asked sadly.

"No party," Josh said absolutely.

There was a knock on the door and Joshua answered it. Andrew stood there in his rain gear ready for school.

"So happy birthday, Joshua," Andrew said. He handed Joshua a small box wrapped in E.T. wrapping paper with green ribbon.

"That's very nice of you, Andrew," Mrs. Bates said.

"The thing is, I'm sort of forgetting my birthday," Josh said.

"How come?" Andrew asked.

"If I stay in third grade much longer, I'll be as old as the teachers," Josh said as he put his bookbag over his shoulder.

"Are you forgetting presents too?" Andrew asked.

"Well . . . " Joshua shook the box Andrew had given him. "I haven't quite decided."

"You'll never guess in a million years what I got you," Andrew said.

"Open it, Josh," Amanda said.

"Please," Andrew said.

"I guess I should since you went to all this trouble."

It was a night light for his dirt bike and he went out to the shed with Andrew to attach it.

"Have you changed your mind about presents now?" Amanda asked, standing beside her brother in the shed.

"Maybe," Joshua said. "Probably so, but no party and I don't want you to tell anyone at school that I'm ten."

Mrs. Goodwin was not in a good humor. She didn't even smile when Joshua arrived at school. After reading class she called him to her desk to say that she was going to cancel tutoring for the rest of the week because of personal complications. Besides, she said, she had to write all the third-grade report cards.

"Report cards?" Josh asked weakly. "I had forgotten about them. I suppose you'll have to write one for me even though I've already been in the third grade once."

"Of course," Mrs. Goodwin said.

"I've had quite a lot of bad news today already, so I don't want to talk about report cards," Joshua said.

"Neither do I."

At recess Mrs. Goodwin asked Joshua to stay after the other children left.

"What kind of bad news have you had today?" she asked.

"It's not a big deal," Josh said, flipping through the spelling tests on her desk.

"We seem to get our bad news on the same day, Josh. Mine is that Mr. Goodwin has filed for divorce." Mrs. Goodwin got up from her desk to write the homework assignment on the blackboard. "Today I feel a hundred years old, too old to teach school any longer—too fat, too wrinkled, too gray haired."

"But you're not."

"I'm not but that's how I feel, so it may as well be true," she said. "And what about your bad news?"

"Well," Joshua said, considering. "Today I'm ten years old."

Mrs. Goodwin began to smile. Her lips turned up, her eyes curved, her skin turned pink, and she began to laugh out loud. She reached over and hugged Joshua hard.

"Is that your terrible news?" she asked.

"Don't tell anyone," Joshua said fiercely.

"I won't tell a soul," Mrs. Goodwin said.

All day on October 11 no one said anything to Joshua about his birthday.

"The fourth graders have probably forgotten," Josh said to Andrew on the playground.

"I didn't think you wanted anyone to know," Andrew said.

"I don't," Joshua said, "but it seems strange to be ten and not ten at the same time."

The afternoon crawled by so slowly, Joshua thought it would never end. Reading went on and on. Sports was cancelled because of rain. There was a movie about lions but the film snapped on the first reel, so the third graders had an extra library period.

"I told my family to forget my birthday," Joshua told Mrs. Goodwin at the end of the school day.

"No presents?"

"Well, maybe, since I let them know so late. But no party."

He copied down his homework assignment, picked up his books, and got up to leave.

"Thanks for not telling anyone," he said to Mrs. Goodwin as he left.

Andrew had already left when Joshua got downstairs. Amanda had piano lessons. He stopped at People's Drugs and played four extra games of Pac Man wishing the day would hurry on to October 12 so he wouldn't have to think about cancelling his birthday. He got a double-dip maple walnut cone, two packs of baseball cards, a new *Dr. Strange* comic, and a rubber doll that wet her pants for Georgianna.

He looked at the clock over the newsstand and it was only four o'clock. His mother wouldn't be home from her exercise class until five.

From the pay phone outside People's Drugs he called Andrew, but Andrew was at a friend's house and wouldn't be back until after dinner. He called Mrs. Goodwin and to his great surprise nobody answered the telephone. In desperation, he called his father's office, but the secretary said his father had left at three and was not expected back. Mr. Bates was a very regular man and never left his office at three o'clock. At least, Joshua thought, if he went home Plutarch would be sleeping on the living room sofa. Already it was dark as night outside and Joshua was beginning to think he would die of loneliness.

All the lights were off in the house when Joshua arrived and opened the front door, but there was a strange and wonderful sweet smell in the hall and he sensed that he was not alone.

"Plutarch," he called absently, although he knew perfectly well that Plutarch never came when he was called. "Mama?" But there was no answer.

He went straight upstairs to his room, dropped his bookbag on his desk, fed his goldfish, and went back down to the kitchen. He was just opening the freezer door to check for yogurt sticks when he heard Amanda's voice from the living room and then his mother's and then his father's.

"Happy birthday to you, happy birthday to you, happy birthday, dear Joshua, happy birthday to you."

And when he went into the living room, his heart beating like a small drum, the room was full of balloons and streamers in every color of the rainbow and a poster saying HAPPY BIRTHDAY, DEAR JOSHUA, HOWEVER OLD YOU CHOOSE TO BE.

The coffee table was stacked with presents and there in the middle was a large chocolate birthday cake.

"All day I've been afraid you really wouldn't have a party," Joshua said.

"Well, we did," Mrs. Bates said happily.

Eight

One afternoon Joshua's first-quarter report card was on the radiator on top of the rest of the mail when he came home from school to get his bike. He picked up the familiar brown envelope with the intention of opening it right away before his mother came home from the market with Georgianna. But just the feel of the envelope in his hand filled him with the terrors of his failures in past years. He dropped the envelope behind the radiator.

"You got your report card," Amanda called from the living room, where she was sitting in the rocker reading her own report. Joshua didn't answer. He went into the kitchen, took a raspberry yogurt stick from the freezer, and started out the back door to the shed where he kept his dirt bike.

"Bye," he called as he left, not anxious for a conversation with brilliant Amanda.

"Don't you want to read your report?" Amanda asked, following him.

"Mine isn't there," he said quickly.

"I saw it when I came home. It was just under mine."

"Well, it's not there now," he said, exiting quickly. "How many subjects did you flunk?"

"I got a B in language arts."

"Big deal," Josh said. "If you're not careful, you'll be held back."

And he rode down Wisconsin Avenue to R Street as fast as his bike would go.

Mrs. Goodwin was packing book boxes when he arrived. The small house was full of the sweet smell of sugar cookies baking, and on the floor of the living room next to the boxes of books, the boa constrictor slithered back and forth in its glass aquarium.

"So," Mrs. Goodwin said, as she sealed a box with masking tape. "Mr. Goodwin is finally going to be moving his things out of the house—on Halloween night, of all times."

Joshua followed her into the kitchen, where she took a tray of sugar cookies out of the oven and gave one to Joshua while it was still soft and hot.

"Are you going to be divorced immediately?" he asked.

"I suppose we are. Mr. Goodwin hasn't told me his plans. Only that he wants to live alone."

She sat down next to Joshua and opened *The Joy of Reading: 4* to a story about a boy and his grandfather.

"I suppose it's just as difficult to be a grownup as it is to be a child," Joshua said.

"Sometimes it is. This year for example," Mrs. Goodwin said as she settled down next to him.

"At least you don't flunk," Joshua said.

"That's not necessarily true. There're all kinds of flunking."

That afternoon they read story after story, until Joshua, full to the brim with cookies and hot chocolate and love for Mrs. Goodwin, was reading with as much ease as anyone in fourth grade could possibly read.

Afterward he helped Mrs. Goodwin pack book boxes and move the furniture which the movers would be taking to Mr. Goodwin's house. In one box Mrs. Goodwin packed two pictures from the library and took a photograph of her two sons when they were small off the desk to pack.

"Jonathan was exactly your age there," she said, handing the photgraph to Joshua. "He was terrible in school. I had to go in to see his third-grade teacher every week. He couldn't spell. He refused to learn his multiplication tables. And now he's a doctor."

She put the photograph in the box with the pictures.

"You won't be in the third grade forever," she said, ruffling Joshua's hair. "Did you get your report card?"

Joshua hesitated.

"Well, it should be there when you get home," Mrs. Goodwin said. "I think you'll be surprised."

The brown envelope was still behind the radiator when he got home from Mrs. Goodwin's house. He slid it out, tucked it under his T-shirt and went to his bedroom to read it. He was astonished.

He had an A in everything except spelling and reading.

"Joshua is doing excellent work in third grade," Mrs. Goodwin had written. "I plan to give him a standardized test in November just before Thanksgiving. There is a chance, if he does well, that he will be promoted before the end of the year."

"So how'd you say you did in language arts?" he asked Amanda, who was practicing handstands against the front door.

"B. B in math too. And a C-plus in history. It's the worst report I've had in my whole life."

"Bad luck," Joshua said and he went into the dining room, where his mother was putting supper on the table.

"My report card came," he said casually. He lifted Georgianna out of her high chair, and took a bite of the soggy arrowroot cookie in her plump hand.

"Oh good. I hoped it had come," his mother said. "Have you looked at it?"

"Yup," Joshua said, shrugging his shoulders to conceal his great pleasure. "It's not bad."

Nine

By late October the dark mornings of the school day had begun to diminish entirely for Joshua. On Halloween morning he awoke to bright autumn sunlight in his window and realized to his very great surprise that he had slept the night without a nightmare of spelling tests and lost math papers and teachers flying like demons through the open windows of his room; that he didn't have a stomachache for the first time since Labor Day; and when he got out of bed his knees didn't fold like spaghetti beneath him as he anticipated the terrors of another morning at Mirch Elementary.

He looked at himself in the mirror over his

Here

dresser. He was looking quite wonderful, he thought. He tried on his baseball cap so the bill just shaded his eyes and decided he was actually beginning to take on the appearance of a professional baseball player. He could imagine himself at twenty years old playing shortstop for the Orioles.

At breakfast that morning he had seconds on eggs and two pieces of toast.

"Well, Josh, you must be feeling pretty well," Mr. Bates said.

"I'm feeling terrific," Josh said. "Before you know it, I may pass straight through third grade into fourth."

On the morning of Halloween, Tommy Wilhelm came into the third-grade classroom dressed as a pirate with pumpkin cookies from the fourth graders to pass out.

"So how's third grade going second time around?" he asked Joshua.

"Swell," Josh said, not looking up for fear that if he saw a smirk on Tommy Wilhelm's face, he would be inspired to knock it off with his fist.

Mrs. Goodwin, who had been until that very moment correcting math tests at her desk, stood up and motioned Tommy Wilhelm to sit down in the empty desk next to Josh.

"I understand you haven't learned to behave like a fourth grader, so you're going to spend some time in third grade with me."

"That's not true," Tommy said, alarmed. "Nobody told me."

"I'm telling you now," Mrs. Goodwin said. She reached into her bookcase, took out *The Joy of Reading: 3*, and opened it on the desk in front of Tommy.

"I'd like you to read aloud, please."

Tommy began to read, but he was so shaken by the terrible news of his demoting that he halted at every word.

Mrs. Goodwin shook her head sadly.

"I simply don't know how you were promoted from Mrs. Nice's class," she said.

"I got all A's. Well, nearly all A's," Tommy said desperately.

Mrs. Goodwin rolled her eyes. She handed

Tommy a copy of the math test she had given to the third grade that morning.

"Try this for me," she said.

"It's a cinch," Tommy said, and he completed the math test as fast as he could.

When Mrs. Goodwin corrected it, she handed it back with a fat red 60 on the top of the page.

"Not cinchy enough," she said.

Tommy Wilhelm sat in his pirate costume at the desk next to Joshua. He did third-grade social studies and language arts and math. He missed recess with the fourth grade and the Halloween party. By lunch time he was almost in tears.

"Please let me go back to my own class now," he said to Mrs. Goodwin.

She raised her eyebrows but made no response.

"You must be the dumbest boy in the fourth grade," Paulie Soll said.

"I'm smart enough when I'm in my own class," Tommy said.

"We just made up a new rule," Sammy Laser said. "Anyone in third grade for more than one class can't play with fourth graders for a week."

"Please." Tommy Wilhelm, his face as bright as cranberries, looked desperately at Joshua. "Make them lay off."

Joshua looked up from his reading. "How come you need my protection?" he asked.

"I swear on a stack of Bibles I'll never make fun of you again."

"Why should I believe you?"

"Ask Mrs. Goodwin to let me go back to my own class?" Tommy begged.

"Ask her yourself."

"If you let me go back to my class, I promise I'll never bother Josh again for the rest of my life."

"No bargains, Tommy. You'll go back when I'm ready for you to go back."

When the bell rang, Mrs. Goodwin dismissed Tommy from the class first. He had to walk straight across the front of the classroom in front of the whole third grade sitting in dead silence for his departure. Just as the door shut behind him, Paulie Soll, who could see through the glass, reported that Tommy had darted into the boy's room where according to Paulie, he would probably cry his eyes out.

"I doubt you'll have much more real trouble from Tommy," Mrs. Goodwin said to Joshua as he left for lunch.

"Thanks a lot," Joshua said.

When Joshua arrived at Mrs. Goodwin's house on the afternoon of Tommy Wilhelm's humiliation, there was an orange Round the Clock moving van in front of the house and two movers were carrying the red chintz couch out the front door. Mrs. Goodwin stood on the porch holding the glass aquarium with the boa constrictor; a small balding man with a thin-haired mustache was directing the movers.

While Joshua watched, they carried out a bed, a dresser, a rocking chair, the kitchen table, the Chinese rug from the dining room, the large desk from the study, two chairs, boxes and boxes of books, and countless lamps. Then the balding man took the aquarium from Mrs. Goodwin, got in a red Volkswagen with bucket seats, and drove off.

Joshua followed Mrs. Goodwin into the house. She was very quiet. In the living room she looked in the cage of the mother finch at the two finch babies happily pecking at each other. She kneeled down to pet the yellow Labrador, who raised his head and opened one eye but without enthusiasm. In the kitchen she put up a card table where the kitchen table had been and unfolded two chairs.

"So," she said with great tiredness. "Sit down and get to work."

Joshua sat down.

"I didn't make cookies," she said, "because of the move." She poured him a glass of milk and sat down beside him.

She looked suddenly very old, older than his grandmother, centuries old, the way her skin fell in pockets and her eyes, puffy with crying, were lost in the hollow sockets of her head. Joshua felt terrible for her. Instinctively, he leaned against her warm fleshy body with his weight, as if by his touch she could be young again.

Ten

Two days before Thanksgiving vacation, Joshua took the standardized tests in reading, math, and spelling to determine if he was ready to go into fourth grade.

"I've got my fingers crossed," Mrs. Goodwin said when she gave him the tests to take in the library.

He did the tests in a whiz, even the spelling. On the playground at recess he hit a double in softball which Tommy Wilhelm, at shortstop, missed by a mile.

"I quit playing the third-grade team," Tommy said crossly after the game.

"After today I'm not in third grade any longer,"

Joshua said. "I took a test for fourth grade this morning and aced it."

"I'll believe that when I see it," Tommy Wilhelm said.

The next morning Joshua woke up with a familiar sadness. It was a gray November day striped silver with a thin rain and he didn't want to get out of bed and go to school.

"Sick?" Amanda asked, standing in the doorway to his room already dressed for school.

"Homesick," Joshua said out of the blue, but homesick was exactly how he felt.

He had been homesick before. Every September since kindergarten, he was homesick during the first few days of school. And then, the summer he was eight, he had visited his uncle's farm in Michigan for a month. The second his plane took off from Washington National Airport, whizzing over the Potomac River toward Michigan, he had suddenly felt ill with a terrible sadness. For a while after his uncle and cousins met him at the airport in Detroit, he felt better, but as soon as the sun went down at his uncle's farm and Joshua climbed between the covers of his new bed, the sickness came back in waves until he thought he would sink beneath the undertow.

"I feel empty a lot of the time," he wrote to his mother the first week he was in Michigan. "It's as if half of me spilled out somewhere."

"You're homesick," his mother wrote back. "Eventually you'll feel better."

And Joshua did. Every day he was a little stronger, as if he were recovering from a virus.

Then to his great surprise, when the month was over and his uncle took him to the airport in Detroit, the same familiar sadness came over him as the plane took off for Washington. For the first few days back home, he lay around the house without the energy to play ball or ride his dirt bike or even play soldiers by himself.

"I miss the farm," he told his mother.

"I'm sure you do, darling," his mother said.

"I mean I feel homesick for the farm and it's not even my home."

"I know, Josh. Homesickness will probably happen to you a lot in your life—almost every time you have to leave someplace or someone you love."

"Brother," Joshua said. "That's very bad news."

"Josh is homesick," Amanda said at the breakfast table.

Mr. Bates raised his eyebrows.

"For what?" he asked.

Joshua shrugged. "That's how I felt when I woke up this morning."

He couldn't eat his eggs at breakfast, and on the way to school his eyes filled unaccountably with tears.

"Brother Joshua," Amanda said. "What is the matter with you?"

"Beats me," Josh said and skipped a pebble straight across Lowell Street.

He guessed that he was not homesick but sick with fear that he had failed the test.

"So what if you don't pass, Josh," Amanda said, trying to be of some comfort. "It won't be the worst thing in the world."

"The trouble is that right now I don't want to

leave third grade and I don't want to stay there either," Josh said.

Mrs. Goodwin was sitting at her desk correcting the reading assignments when Josh came in. She called hello but she didn't look up as if, he decided, she didn't want to tell him the bad news.

He sat down at his desk, opened his bookbag, and took out a stack of baseball trading cards, but he couldn't concentrate on the players. He read over his book report for second period and his composition on Indian ballgames for social studies. From time to time he glanced at Mrs. Goodwin, who seemed not in the least interested in telling him how he had done on the test for fourth grade.

Maybe, he thought, she hadn't had time to correct it. Or she had just checked his spelling and thrown up her hands in sorrow and frustration at his failure.

"Mrs. Goodwin," he said, unable to wait any longer. "Did you happen to check my test?"

She looked up from her correcting with an expression of real sadness. "Yes, Josh. I corrected it last night and you did wonderfully." She handed him the test booklet to look over. "Better than I ever dreamed you would do."

"So I'm in fourth grade?"

"So you are," she said, careful not to let on how much she would miss him. "Congratulations, Joshua." She shook his hand.

"Congratulations to us both," Josh said.

"So I passed," he said to Amanda on the playground at recess.

"Josh will be in fourth grade after Thanksgiving," Amanda told Tommy Wilhelm.

"I did fifth-grade work on the test," Joshua said cockily.

"Maybe you'll graduate from high school at eleven," Tommy said.

"Brother," Andrew said on the way home. "This is the happiest day in my life."

"I passed," Joshua called to his mother as he burst in the front door of his house.

"Josh pass," Georgianna said happily.

And he sat down at the kitchen table with Plutarch on his lap to celebrate with a hot fudge sundae.

"No more tutoring," he said. "I can play outside all afternoon."

"Or play Pac Man," Amanda said.

"Or ride my bike to Hearst Playground and play softball."

"Just be home at five-thirty as usual," his mother said.

So Joshua put on his rain parka, went to the shed, got his dirt bike, and rode off in the direction of People's Drugs, but he didn't stop at People's. He rode down Wisconsin Avenue at a pace, screeching to a stop at the crossroads, and turned left at R Street. He locked his bike on the familiar birch tree and went up the steps.

Mrs. Goodwin had just settled down with a cup of tea, a piece of chocolate cake, and a Mounds bar when Joshua rang her front door.

"Hello," she said. "I'm very glad to see you."

She poured him a cup of tea and sliced a piece of

cake. Then she pulled up a chair and sat down across from him.

"This morning when I woke up, I was homesick," Joshua said to her.

"You know, Joshua," Mrs. Goodwin said, halving her Mounds bar with him. "So was I."

SUSAN SHREVE is the author of numerous books for young people and adults. Her adult books include *Children of Power* and her most recent, *Dreaming of Heros*. *The Masquerade, Loveletters,* and *The Revolution of Mary Leary,* young adult novels, and *The Nightmares of Geranium Street, Family Secrets,* and *The Bad Dreams of A Good Girl,* for young readers, have all been published by Knopf.

A graduate of the University of Pennsylvania and recipient of a Guggenheim fellowship, Susan Shreve is an associate professor of English at George Mason University and a visiting professor at Columbia University. She lives with her husband and their four children in Washington, D.C.